nick jr.

LEMON PIRATES!

by Mary Man-Kong
illustrated by Dave Aikins

Random House 🏠 New York

It is a hot day.

Top Wing cadets

Rod and Brody

go to the Lemon Shack.

They ask Rhonda
for frozen lemon swirlies.
They want to keep cool.

Rhonda is running low
on lemons!
Brody will race
to the Lemon Coast
to get more.

Cap'n Dilly and Matilda
want to make their own
frozen lemon swirlies.
They plan to take
Brody's lemon treasure!

Brody is happy.
He zooms back
to the Lemon Shack
with Rhonda's lemons.

To stop Brody,
Matilda makes holes
in his Splash Wing.

Now Brody's boat
has a leak.
The Splash Wing
is sinking!

Cap'n Dilly and Matilda
take the lemon treasure.
They leave in their
pirate ship.

Brody needs help!
He presses
the Top Wing button
on his watch.

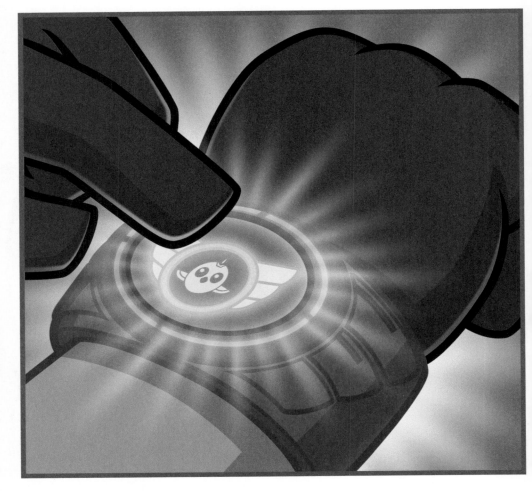

Time for
the Top Wing cadets
to earn their wings!
Penny and Swift will help.

Penny tows
Brody's Splash Wing
to Top Wing Academy's
headquarters.
The boat will get fixed
there.

Swift flies his Flash Wing.
He sees the pirate ship
near some big rocks.

Rod helps, too.

He drives his Road Wing

to the rocks.

But he is too far

from the pirate ship.

Rod has an idea.

With his Road Wing,

he hops from rock to rock

to get to the ship.

He hops right onto the deck.

He cock-a-doodle-*DID* it!

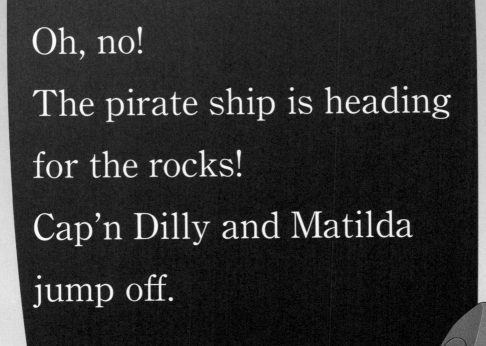

Oh, no!

The pirate ship is heading

for the rocks!

Cap'n Dilly and Matilda

jump off.

Team Top Wing
to the rescue!
Rod steers the ship.

Swift uses his Flash Wing
to move the pirate ship
away from the rocks.
Everyone is safe!

At the Lemon Shack, there are no more lemons to make frozen lemon swirlies.

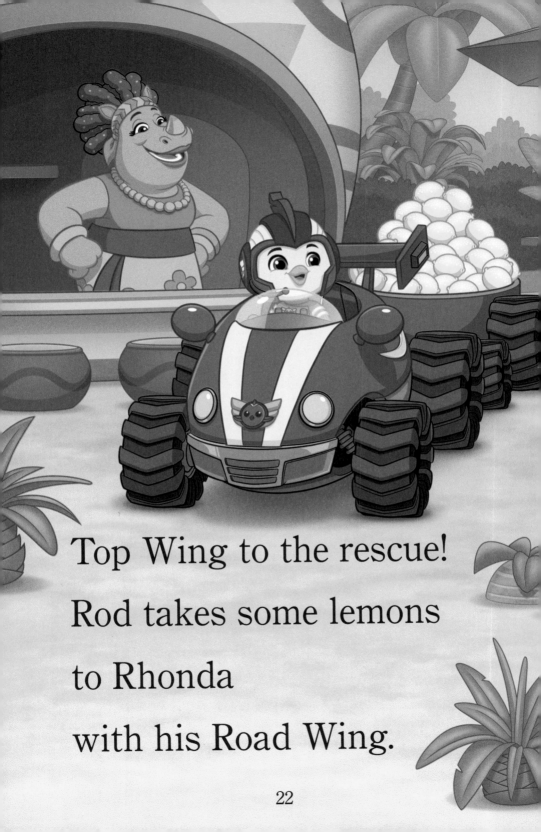

Top Wing to the rescue!
Rod takes some lemons
to Rhonda
with his Road Wing.

Swift drops some
from his Flash Wing.
Lemons for everyone!

Cap'n Dilly and Matilda
ask nicely for drinks.
Rhonda says yes.
Hooray for Top Wing!
Hooray for frozen lemon
swirlies!